Fun House Terrors!

PLOT-IT-YOURSELF
HORROR STORIES™ #6

Fun House Terrors!

by HILARY MILTON

Illustrated by Paul Frame

WANDERER BOOKS
Published by Simon & Schuster, Inc., New York

Copyright © 1984 by Hilary Milton
All rights reserved
including the right of reproduction
in whole or in part in any form
Published by WANDERER BOOKS
A Division of Simon & Schuster, Inc.
Simon & Schuster Building
1230 Avenue of the Americas
New York, New York 10020

Designed by Stanley S. Drate/Folio Graphics Company, Inc.
Manufactured in the United States of America
10 9 8 7 6 5 4 3 2 1

WANDERER and colophon are registered trademarks
of Simon & Schuster, Inc.

Also available in Julian Messner library edition

PLOT IT YOURSELF HORROR STORIES is a registered trademark of Simon & Schuster, Inc.

Library of Congress Cataloging in Publication Data

Milton, Hilary H.
   Fun house terrors!

   (Plot it yourself horror stories #6)
   Summary: The reader visits a seaside amusement park
where the rides turn out to be more terrifying than
amusing; the reader makes choices which determine the
outcome of the plot.
   1. Plot-your-own stories. 2. Children's stories,
American. [1. Horror stories. 2. Amusement parks—
Fiction. 3. Plot-your-own stories] I. Frame, Paul,
1913–   , ill. II. Title. III. Series.
PZ7.M6447Fu 1984   [Fic]   84-7374
ISBN: 0-671-52406-2
ISBN: 0-671-53041-0 (lib. bdg.)

BEWARE!

Riptide Wonders is no ordinary amusement park. In fact, the moment you set foot inside the park, you won't be so much amused as scared out of your wits.

The park is filled with unspeakable horrors! You will struggle desperately to survive. Don't be fooled, however, as every time you think you're safe, a new and terrifying choice will have to be made.

Will you:

Be trapped by an evil witch?

Become a meal for man-eating plants?

Survive a crash landing on the terrifying Drop-Off ride?

Be eaten by vicious alligators?

Or, become one of the exhibits in the wax museum?

Remember your fate is in your own hands. Only you can decide whether you'll make it through the many hair-raising tales in FUN HOUSE TERRORS!

You and seven of your schoolmates have just spent two days at the Kennedy Space Center, watching a spectacular launch of the Challenger Space Shuttle. You're there with Mr. Howe, your science teacher, and Mrs. Howe, the school librarian. The trip is an honor you and your friends have earned by writing special study papers.

You've all come down from Nashville on a small school bus, but you have two more days before you have to be back home. Mr. and Mrs. Howe suggest that you drive up the west coast of Florida, stop near Pensacola, and enjoy the beach.

You stop at a motel called Windward Surf and spend all day enjoying the sand and water. After dinner, Mr. Howe says he'll take four students into Pensacola to the movies. Mrs. Howe says she wants to see some large boats, so she rents a car and the rest of you pile in with her.

On the way to the marina, though, you keep seeing signs advertising an amusement park called Riptide Wonders. You see pictures of unusual rides, of clowns and freaks, and of a well-lighted midway with all sorts of arcades and concessions. The closer you get to the park, the more interesting the billboards make it seem.

Turn to page 2

2

As you approach a junction you see the largest billboard you've ever seen. It has lights flickering on and off, reminding you of the movement of a roller coaster.

You lean over and tap Mrs. Howe's shoulder. "If you don't mind," you say, "I'd like to stop here and see all those things."

"By yourself?" She's not sure about leaving you alone.

But you convince her you'll be all right. You've seen signs that tell you buses come along every hour going back to where the motel is. You can catch one of those. "Besides," you tell her, "I'm not much on boats."

She lets you off, first making sure you have enough money to try a couple of rides, then buy your bus ticket. "But be in by ten o'clock," she says. "We have to get an early start home tomorrow."

You agree and get out. You think either Janie or Thomas will come with you but neither does. But you don't care, you can go it alone.

At the entrance to Riptide Wonders you pick up a folder that describes some of the fun houses and rides, five of which carry you out over the Gulf of Mexico.

You read about the Mad Dog roller coaster, the Ski Glide hang glider, the Paratroop Plunge parachute ride, the Pier Flipper, and the Sky Chase cable car ride, all of which go out over the water. You feel goose bumps along your arms as you read about them.

Turn to page 3

3

Riptide Wonders also has a House of Mirrors, a Wax Museum, a Swamp Jungle, whatever that is, and a House of Horrors. It all sounds like good scary fun.

Once inside the park, you wander down the midway, glancing at the game concessions, the little snack bars, and the entrances to the walk-in attractions. You see the section of kiddie rides but you're too big for those. They're *too* safe.

At the fenced-off area surrounding the ferris wheel, you stare up at the device. It's different from those you've ridden before—the seats seem to move in three directions. There's the giant armlike part that goes around a center axis while the seats go up and down along a different path. Also, the seats revolve as the arm moves in a high arc. And half of it hangs out over the Gulf when the huge arm is extended horizontally.

As you watch, the machine stops momentarily and you hear all the riders scream. Those on the outermost seats are suspended over rippling, white-capped waves.

But what are they afraid of? The machine won't break!

You stare a moment longer, then you reach a fork in the path you've been following. Go right, and you'll be at the largest merry-go-round you've ever seen. Go left, and you'll enter the fascinating House of Mirrors.

If you choose to try the merry-go-round, turn to page 10. But if you prefer the House of Mirrors, turn to page 4.

4

After a moment of uncertainty, you select the House of Mirrors. You buy your ticket and start toward the entrance. But just as you reach it and are about to walk inside, you hear a scream. You look back. A giant of a man, wearing a silvery costume and a horrid mask that remind you of outer space movies, has lifted a woman high above his head and seems about to throw her into the Gulf. Part of the show, you realize, but it's frightening just the same.

You look past the creature and see three other costumed people—one dressed as a clown, one dressed as a terrifying witch, and the third, a broad-shouldered, strong-armed midget, dressed as a horrid troll or elf.

You shiver, then you turn quickly into the House of Mirrors.

You walk slowly along, glancing right and left at the brightly lighted walls until suddenly you bang into something solid. *This* mirror so perfectly hides the hall that you're completely fooled by it. You hesitate a moment, take two backward steps, then turn left. At that instant, all the bright lights go out and only a faint glow reflects from some small candlelike bulbs.

You don't know whether to turn or go straight.

Turn? Which way? Go to page 13.
If you choose to go straight, turn to page 22.

You're terrified. You know sharks sometimes come close to shore. But this thing is round, like a pole. You grab on to it and are rapidly pulled out of the water.

5

You cling with all your might, blinking away the salty water that's blurring your vision. When you can finally see, you realize you've caught one of the Pier Flipper's rotating spokelike arms. Much to your relief, there's a seat at the end of it! You twist about and flop onto it. And just in time, for the wheel keeps turning. It carries you up and up. You laugh, you're so relieved. But your laughter dies when you look around and discover you're the only rider . . .

Before you have time to wonder why, the wheel shudders, then comes to a sudden halt, with you at the very top. The little engine that makes it move begins to shake. You think the chair is going to break off the spokelike arm.

But it does not break free. It remains dangling at the end of the support arm. Still, you think the arm is stronger, so you grab it with both hands and wrap your legs around it. You slide down, much as you might let yourself down a tall flagpole. But you're only halfway to the rails when the arm shakes violently, then cracks—and seems about to fling you out into the water!

You're bracing for the splash when you feel the thing suddenly stop, with you in midair.

Turn to page 49.

6

For a moment the trembling stops and you are about to believe it was all in your imagination. But it begins once more, and this time it's even more violent.

They ought to call this place something else besides the House of Mirrors!

The shaking becomes so violent you're sure you're going to fall. Instinctively, you reach out for the closest mirror wall—only to discover that it is not there! What you actually see is the reflection of a reflection.

You stumble, trip, and fall headlong. The floor is now shaking so hard you're sure the building is going to come tumbling down about you. Frantically you flail your arms, fingers reaching for something to grab on to. You touch something that feels like the edge of a baseboard and you grasp it with all your might.

And just at that moment, the walls seem to erupt.

Horrified, you think of terrible storms or earthquakes. You've never read of earthquakes in Florida, but maybe there's a first time for everything.

You take a deep breath, trying to get to your feet, when all of a sudden the whole building seems to explode.

Turn to page 26.

7

You start to pull your arm away, but those claw-tipped fingers suddenly wrap themselves around your wrist. And the claws poke into your flesh like dull knife points.

You try to pull free—first easily, then harder, and finally with all your might. But you cannot.

Again the creature laughs. "Having fun?" The voice is high-pitched and it reminds you of those horrid vampire creatures you've seen in TV cartoons.

The Triple Spin seems suddenly to go faster—up and down, around, back and forth. And you don't like it you don't like it at all.

"I just want to get off!" You holler.

The creature throws back its weird head and the laughter sounds terribly wild. "Oh, *nobody* ever gets off the Triple Spin!"

Turn to page 39.

8

You bang into it with all the force you can muster. Instantly, it goes silent and totters on the pedestal. You fall back but you've already committed yourself so you bang into it once more, harder this time. And when you do, the head rolls to the edge, seems to balance itself there for a moment, and then teeters and drops to the floor.

Instantly, all the other heads become still. Not a sound. Then, as if on signal, they begin screaming, "Catch the kid! Catch the kid! Catch-the-kid-catch-the-kid-catch-the-kid!"

Trembling, you bend your knees, set yourself, and leap up and onto the platform. Instantly it begins to shake, leaning first right, then left.

Can you leap for the holes in the canvas top? Turn to page 69.
Or does something happen to prevent your escape? Turn to page 55.

Once you're out of the smoke-filled House of Mirrors, you cough, then breathe deeply. You nod to yourself—no thanks, no more going into these amusement houses or whatever they are. You know you made a mistake—best turn around, walk back out the gate, and return to the motel. You're really too tired to enjoy all these rides, anyway.

You start to take a step to the right, but just then the wide platform you're standing on makes a quick, jerky upward move. Wildly, you reach out to brace yourself, and grab a steel postlike handle.

And just in time, for the platform stops jerking and suddenly whisks you up and up and up—and higher!

Frantically, you look up and you do *not* like what you see!

Turn to page 28.

10

After only a moment's hesitation, you decide that first you'll try a ride, so you take the right fork. You buy your ticket and wait till the machine stops for a new load of passengers. While you wait your turn, you stare at the objects to be ridden.

Most merry-go-rounds have horses or ponies, some with small benches for people who don't want to go up and down. But these saddled things are different—because, you suppose, this amusement park is so close to the Gulf. You see a hammerhead shark, three dolphins, something that looks like an octopus, two huge squids, a weird-looking fish that must be a stingray, and four sea turtles.

While waiting your turn, you decide which creature to ride.

If you select a turtle ride, turn to page 51.
But if the squid seems more interesting, turn to page 58.

You think you spot a hallway to your left. Hesitating only a second, you give your head a quick nod and start running that way. But you take only six steps when you bang hard into a huge mirror! You turn right—and again bang into smooth, reflecting glass!

Once more you scream! And you do more—you kick as hard as you can at the closest mirror. It shatters into innumerable fragments and slivers and appears to open a way of escape. You scurry through the hole you've made, being careful to duck and avoid the jagged edges.

On the other side, sure enough, there appears to be a narrow hall, just wide enough for you to squeeze through. But the smoke is getting thicker and you wonder if you'll be able to get out before you're either overcome by the fumes or caught up in the blaze.

You get halfway down the hall and are sure you see the outside. But suddenly, when you're less than ten feet from the end, it's blocked—by one of the characters you saw in the park's midway, the one dressed like a witch.

Does the witch offer help? Turn to page 24.
Or is this some kind of trap? Turn to page 31.

12

You stare for a moment, then slowly you begin to retreat. Although you have not looked at every wall in the room, you know there has to be a door somewhere.

The ape-man head turns right and left, although it never takes its gaze from your face. It repeats itself: "Catch the kid!"

And like a chorus, all the other heads join in: *"Catch the kid! Catch the kid!"*

Those voices, some shrill, some deep and rumbling, send cold chills up and down your spine. You *did not* come to Riptide Wonders to be frightened, certainly not to be *caught!* But as these heads with their horrid expressions and staring eyes all turn and face you, you fear them.

You try to control your movements, don't want to let the weird things think you're scared, as you pivot slowly, your gaze sweeping each wall. Two seem to be blank, and one of them has the huge door through which the box was brought in. The fourth, you cannot guess where it leads, is directly behind the largest head.

You think that if you dash through the door where the box was brought in, whoever brought you here will be waiting. So you have to use another exit, *if* you can find one.

Turn to page 53.

13

While trying to make up your mind, you glance down, squinting your eyes, hoping you can make out some kind of mirror frame or baseboard—anything that will give you a hint about which direction to take. You think you spot a bulge in the carpet, like the one in the corner of your bedroom. That has to be a hint; you'll make a turn to the left.

You do so, and within seconds you're confronted by a horribly distorted reflection of yourself. You look like an overblown basketball in the middle, with very short arms and legs, no neck, and just a little round dot for a head. You stare at the reflection, and as you do so, it gradually starts to shrink.

Turn to page 15.

Then, suddenly, the image disappears!

You almost jump at the abrupt change. You try to laugh at yourself. Well, why can't the reflection change? After all, this is a fun house.

15

You sniff and shift your gaze to the mirror on the opposite side, and you are horror-stricken!

Why? Do you see something that should not be there? Turn to page 33.

Do you see a more frightening reflection? Turn to page 21.

But wait—maybe you see a somebody! Turn to page 29.

16

It's cold and slippery and very smooth. And when your fingers wrap around it, the thing seems to have a life of its own. You let out a little cry and jerk it away. Limply, it falls to the floor. You stare at it for a moment, then you squat down and examine it closely.

And you almost laugh at yourself. It's a long strip of rubberlike material, the kind a builder might use for insulating a window, or maybe to hold a large plate-glass mirror firmly in place.

Relieved, you stand, then proceed once more down the hallway of the House of Mirrors. For a short distance, the walls seem only to reflect you as you really are. And you think you're on your way, or at least, on the right path. But just when you think everything will go all right for the rest of the way, you bang solidly into a mirror you hadn't expected—and have to turn.

But which way?

You're trying to make up your mind, when suddenly the floor begins to tremble.

You catch your breath. Is the House of Mirrors vibrating? Or is there something more to this place, something besides the reflecting walls?

Turn to page 6.

17

You're standing on a narrow platform. You pause and take a deep breath and start to run forward. But something inside you makes you hesitate just long enough to look down . . .

And you find yourself at the end of a pier that has no safety rail. Another step and you'll fall headfirst into the rolling waves.

You spin about and the witch creature is standing well behind you, safely on the beach, laughing a shrill, cackling laugh.

You don't like it one bit! All you want to do is have a good time—never mind being scared half to death! Or getting drowned. You glance once at the House of Mirrors, then you start back toward the area of rides. But just as you step off the pier, the witch creature suddenly grabs you and throws you across its back—and you *know* that if it's a woman, she's the strongest one you've ever met.

You try to turn yourself around, get free. But her fingers are too strong!

She carries you past the snack and concession stands, past the merry-go-round and across the midway to the Gravity Whip—a whirling machine with chairs hanging from long chains.

Turn to page 100.

18

You think it wants to hold your hand but you don't like those claws! So you pretend to grab on to the seat, hoping the creature will leave you alone. And anyway, you don't want to ride this device, whatever it is. All you want to do is get off.

The troll seems to guess what you're thinking. It throws back its head and laughs. You guess it's supposed to be a laugh, but it's the strangest sound you've ever heard—a cross between the howl of a wolf and the whimper of a small dog. "Off! Off!" it chatters. "Everybody wants to get off." The voice is high-pitched and frightening. You look quickly at the creature's face, then look away.

You should not have done that, for you seem to have angered it. The voice changes to a kind of throaty growl. "I'll get you off!"

You swallow hard and spin around. You don't like the sudden new sound; it tells you the creature does not mean to be kind or gentle.

The seat you're on swings back and forth, and when you look up, you realize that you're almost at the top of the ride. Within seconds, you'll start going down once more. And the thought gives you a sudden inspiration. You can pretend you don't mind. If this thing wants to help, you'll let it think you'll be grateful.

But that means letting those claws touch your hand.

Turn to page 101.

19

You know the walls and ceilings are mirrors, but the image reminds you of a long tunnel that gets narrower and lower as you move into it. And the passageway seems to go downhill.

You stop and extend your hand. You don't touch anything but you *know* something has to be there! Cautiously, you slide your foot forward. It does not bump into a mirror or frame. You hesitate a moment, then you ease the other foot forward. Just as it touches the floor, the mirror wall to your left trembles. You see a vibrating reflection, and the whole side appears to open up and, before you can stop yourself, you stumble and fall in that direction. A weird humming noise comes from just below you. Strange rumbling sounds echo through the hall.

Has something gone wrong with the controls that operate the lights and mirrors of this place? Turn to page 38. Or is the house built over the Gulf of Mexico—and waves are shaking it? Turn to page 30.

20

You open your eyes and look down—to see the earth rushing up to meet you! But just when you're going to crash to your death in this horrid chair, the guide rails make a sharp bend, sending you and the chair along another path, this time parallel to and just above the sandy beach!

You're about to breathe a sigh of relief. You'll coast along for a short distance, then the stopping devices will catch the chair at the getting-off point—

Except you *do not slow down!* You go even faster!

You hear screams and look about. Men and women are wildly waving at you and screaming, "Jump! Jump out!"

You try to move, but you cannot! Gravity and the bent safety bar pin you down!

You whiz past the men and women, past a crowd of horrified beach strollers. Just then you hear more pieces of metal break and the chair leaves the rails!

It goes flying out of the amusement park, over the wide beach, above the frothing, white-capped waves . . .

And you splash down into the Gulf of Mexico!

The chair sinks quickly. You turn, trying to get free. But the safety bar, horribly bent, will not budge. You're pinned there!

And you know . . . as you sink . . . that you'll never make it . . . back to the Riptide Wonders Amusement Park . . . or to the motel . . .

THE END

It's another mirror, all right, and you see your own reflection. But you also see something very frightening indeed. It's the reflection of a giant octopus! The sight leaves you frozen with fear. You've read sea stories of what those horrible-looking creatures can do. Those eight tentacles can wrap around almost anything, and even if one tentacle gets cut off from the body, the rest still cling. And they're hard to kill. Even if one got stabbed or shot in the heart, two more hearts keep pumping blood through the body.

But why? Why is that monstrous creature reflected beside you . . . ?

Before the question can be fully formed, your gaze shifts to one of the tentacles. It moves up. It seems to be slipping itself slowly about your waist.

And just as it appears to be doing so, you feel something cold and wet touching your neck.

Turn to page 36.

22

For the moment, you're uncertain. You think about turning around, checking the way you've come and returning to the entrance to wait there until they have the lights back on. Then you realize that the low lights are part of the plan. You're *not* supposed to see very well. That makes the place more frightening.

You gather up courage and start forward, easing your foot ahead, testing to see whether you bump into another mirror. You don't, so you walk a little faster.

When you come to a slight bend to the right, you stop abruptly. For there, just beyond the bend, you spot a mirror that ripples your reflection—your legs seem very short, your torso looks like it's ten feet high, and your head seems almost as flat as a platter. Your eyes are horribly distorted.

You gasp, turn away, and find yourself staring into a very different kind of reflection.

Turn to page 19.

Your arms and legs flail through the air and you do cartwheels as you fly. For a moment you're sure you're going out over the Gulf, but when you look down you see you're falling on top of one of those round air-filled fun houses where little children play.

It's like a gigantic ball, bigger than your living room at home. And it'll be soft, so you won't be hurt when you land . . .

But wait!

Maybe you won't be hurt, but it *is* like a rubber ball. If you fall on top of it, maybe it'll simply collapse for a moment, then pop up again like any other ball—sending you flying once more!

Unless you can grab on to something as soon as you touch down.

You set yourself, try to control your arms, and just as you touch the surface of the air house you start to grab.

Your fingers slip over the smooth surface but cling to nothing at all! You cry out and clutch wildly, for anything you can catch. Again, you fail, and you know that as soon as you stop sinking down, you'll spring right back up.

Turn to page 94.

24

"This way, this way!" the creature croaks. "I'll lead you to safety!"

You're not sure about following the witch, but right now all you want is to get out of this terrifying House of Mirrors!

At the witch's bidding, you turn left into a narrow, low hallway barely inches taller than you; the witch has to stoop to keep its head from bumping. Smoke seems to be seeping through cracks in the wall and floor and you have to gasp for breath.

By the time you come to the end of the hallway, your eyes are burning and you're sure you're going to choke. But just as you step through a narrow passage, the smoke suddenly disappears. You stop, rub your eyes, and look around. You'd hoped the hallway would lead you outside . . .

But what you see is *not* the outside!

Instead of leading you to safety, the witch has tricked you. You do not understand how such a room could be attached to the House of Mirrors, but here it is, a horrid storehouse of the most frightening sea creatures you've ever seen!

Turn to page 43.

His heavy feet make thump-thump-thumping noises as he walks to the farthest end of the midway. You start to squirm, but he just chuckles and his fingers dig into you more tightly.

Just at the outer edge of the bright lights he turns, and you glance up. He's approaching one of those tall observation towers with bright lights at the top of it. You *do not* want to go up there, but you're powerless to stop him.

The giant creature shifts you, slips you under his arm, and proceeds up the steps. You try to count them—ten, twelve—fifteen, twenty—thirty-five, forty-seven—sixty-three—seventy-four—eighty-nine—one hundred ten.

You don't believe it—one hundred and ten steps to the top. And the giant creature isn't even breathing hard.

He walks out onto a narrow platform and slowly he lifts you high over his head.

"Don't! Put me down!"

He laughs, but the sound has no merriment to it.

Just then you see lights flick back and forth at the end of a long fishing pier. You vaguely see a man moving from the end toward shore, then back again. His fishing rod is extended, and he's clearly trying to land a huge fish.

Then you hear the shout from others on the pier: "A hammerhead! He's hooked a hammerhead shark!"

Turn to page 96.

26

Before you can do anything else, you're suddenly blasted up and out of the House of Mirrors!

You fly in an arc over the merry-go-round, over something called a Gravity Whip, and crash land in the seat of something that's very much like a ferris wheel. You think the brochure called it the Triple Spin. The whole thing goes around over a central axis, some sort of chain device moves the chairs up and down, back and forth, and the chairs, themselves, revolve.

You had no intention of riding this thing. But there's nothing you can do about it now: you're on it and it's moving up and down, around and around.

You think for a moment you're about to be thrown out, so you grab for the long safety bar that's supposed to hold you in. And just as you do, you hear a high-pitched laugh.

You spin about and find you're sitting beside one of those costumed creatures you saw earlier, the very short one that looked like an elf.

Except now it looks like a ferocious troll.

The creature laughs and holds out its hand to you—a hand that's green, with long, bony fingers and short claws at the end, claws that remind you of a gigantic bird's.

Does the troll help you get safely down? Turn to page 18.
Or does he dump you out while you're at the top of the ride? Turn to page 7.

28

Straight up above you is a platform that must be at least two hundred feet in the air. A huge, lighted sign calls it the Drop-Off.

Drop-off! You think you know what that means. You ride slowly up to the top, then you sit on something like the seat of a ferris wheel, and then some kind of catch is released and you fall straight down.

Like an elevator with no brakes or cables!

And you do not think that will be any fun!

You ride higher and higher, clutching the handle pole with all your might. You look down, and the people at the amusement park look like little dolls. Even the huge ferris wheel—you think they call it the Mad Dog—looks like some kind of erector set toy.

You close your eyes, wishing you'd gone with Mrs. Howe to see the boats. But the platform keeps rising and rising. Then all of a sudden it jerks to an abrupt stop. You're so shaken by the suddenness that you yell out. But you know this thing won't carry you back down; you'll have to transfer to that Drop-Off seat.

Very gingerly, you transfer yourself to it, sit down, lock the safety bar—and again close your eyes.

And down you go? Turn to page 41.
Or are you stuck at the top of the tower? Turn to page 48.

29

You see a *somebody,* all right! You see yourself! It's the "thing" you saw in the other mirror moments ago, except it's no longer just a reflection. It's a real object. Did you think your head completely disappeared? It didn't, but now it's no larger than a ping-pong ball sitting on top of a huge round, dressed basketball . . . with fingers . . . your fingers . . . and feet . . . your feet . . . sticking out at the sides and bottom. And that horribly shrunken head-thing, with your eyes, your mouth, your nose, and your hair—it's coming at you.

You step away, glancing to the opposite mirror once more, and there, instead of your own reflection, you see half a dozen things like the first one, all moving toward you!

House of Mirrors? This has to be the original House of Horrors! And you're caught up in it! You do not like it. All you can think of is getting out of here. But how? Which way?

You hesitate only a second, then you make up your mind. You turn toward the single creature—it's easier, you think, to get away from one of them than six—and you take a quick step in that direction. The thing stops.

You take another step. The thing retreats. You squat, stick your finger out at it, and scream.

Does it disappear? Turn to page 97.
Or does it do something totally unexpected? Turn to page 112.

30

You reach for what you expect to be the nearest mirror but find, instead, a peculiar handlelike piece of metal. You pull it . . .

And instantly fall through a trapdoor!

A trapdoor? This is no place for such a thing! But as you fall straight down, you have no time to wonder why. Frantically, you grab for anything you can. But before you can save yourself, you stop abruptly—and find yourself in another dimly lighted hallway. Here there are no mirrors.

You slowly stand up and stare all around. And you discover that somehow you've gotten into another part of the amusement park. It must be a new attraction, one that isn't yet open to the public. But as your gaze shifts from one exhibit to another, you're so fascinated you forget the House of Mirrors. For you're in a wide, long hall, with collections of huge seashells on either side of you. Varicolored lights, flicking on and off, give the whole display an eerie appearance.

You move slowly, staring from one shell to another. They range in color from almost pure white to solid black, but the prettiest are the pink ones with blue or light green insides.

You reach a turn in the hallway and see a sign calling attention to THE WORLD'S LARGEST SHELL. You're staring at the sign when you hear horrid scratching noises coming from just ahead.

From the huge shell? Turn to page 111.
Or is there someone—or something—else in the hall?
Turn to page 104.

"This way!" the creature hollers. "Come this way to safety!"

You cannot tell whether it's a man's or woman's voice, it's so muffled by the disguise. But you're not going to argue—all you want to do is get out of the mirror hall.

You dart in the direction the creature indicates. To your relief, you take only another dozen steps, and you're outside.

But outside to what?

Onto the platform of one of the many rides? Turn to page 9.
Or into the frothing waves of the outgoing tide? Turn to page 17.

32

You hated being closed up in that box, but it was a lot safer there than in this room full of talking heads. You stare at the half-ape, half-man head for one brief second, and its huge mouth opens wide. Those teeth terrify you and now you *know* being in the box is safer.

You spin about and scurry back to it. You lift the lid, clamber over the edge, and drop back inside. The lid slams shut and you hear a click. It's locked!

And that's more frightening, you think, than those heads.

You feel about in the dark, hoping one of the box's ends has a latch or loose board, some way of escaping. But you discover nothing. You hesitate a moment, sniff, and decide that you'll just have to relax and wait for that giant to come release you. After all, if he's part of the amusement park, he's just giving you a special thrill.

After several moments you think you hear his footsteps and you're about to breathe a sigh of relief. "Let me out!" you yell.

But even as the echoes of your cry die away, you hear little scratching sounds. And they're not coming from across the room—they're *very* near you. They're at the ends of the box and on its top.

Turn to page 113.

You see water! At first, you think it's some strange kind of reflection, something that is part of this crazy House of Mirrors. But as you stare at it, you realize that it is *real* water. You take a step back, but you bump into a moving mirror, and before you can stop yourself, you're slapped forward—and into the water.

33

It does *not* make any sense! You're just having a good time looking at reflections and all of a sudden you're getting wet!

Well, you'll just have to walk through the water to the outside; it has to be flowing from the outside. Then you'll go on the rides. You should have done that first, anyway.

Forgetting the mirrors, you walk forward and discover you are now wading. And your sneakers are getting soggy!

You start to hurry, but all of a sudden you stop. It's not just water you've stepped in—this is another part of the amusement park. You now realize getting out won't be easy. Somehow you've gotten yourself into the so-called Tunnel of Love.

Tunnel of Love! You want no part of it. Not walking, anyway. Maybe riding one of those little boats through it would be all right, but wading . . .

Turn to page 85.

34

It's being dragged over the rough ground. And you have to fall against the side of it to keep from getting your face smashed.

You yell. You beat against the sides. You holler for somebody to rescue you. After all, you came to Riptide Wonders to have a good time, not to be locked up in a huge box.

After less than half a minute, the bumping stops. Although the box is still being dragged, now it's on a smoother surface. And after no more than a minute longer, it stops moving altogether. You wait several seconds, then cautiously raise the lid.

The sight that confronts you makes you shiver all over.

Are you about to go on another wild ride? Turn to page 50.
Or is this some kind of crazy house? Turn to page 60.

Without thinking much about it, you make your way to the passage, shove the canvas curtain aside, take three steps forward—and fall onto a pile of damp cardboard boxes.

Instantly, the scratching noise you heard earlier starts again—this time getting louder and louder. You turn, trying to get up, but your hand bumps into one of the boxes. It's so damp it tears, and before you can make another move, you feel something like large tweezers clamp on your finger.

You scream and kick at the box. But your foot knocks another hole in it. More "tweezers" clamp on your ankle. Once more you yell. You squirm about, trying to get to your feet. But every time you move, you knock holes in other boxes—and more "tweezers" clamp on to you.

And then, as you jerk about, you see what's pinching you—the cardboard boxes contain huge lobsters and sea crabs!

Who wants to see shells like those!

You don't know—they've got no business at an amusement park—but they're here. And you *do not* like them.

But they like you!

You holler. You kick your legs and swing your arms. But these live shells don't stop. You try to slap and kick them away. But there are too many, too many. They tear at you and tear at you . . . and tear . . . at . . . you . . .

THE END

36

You let out a war-whoop cry and jump to the left. The thing seems to cling to you. You remember how a real octopus clings to an object; it has little vacuumlike pads at the ends of its tentacles, and they can stick so hard a victim can't jerk free.

You take one more hard look at the mirror, but the reflection has suddenly disappeared! In its place you think you see rolling, swishing stormy sea waves.

That cannot be!

But that's what it looks like. And even as you stare, you feel your feet getting wet.

Something is terribly wrong in this House of Mirrors! You're supposed to be walking along a straight, dry hallway with unexpected turns and angles. But water?

A cold object seems to move over your neck and wrap itself around you. You frantically grab for it and touch something that has no place in a house of mirrors!

A real octopus tentacle? Turn to page 46.
Or some kind of amusement park gimmick? Turn to page 16.

38

You hold your breath, listening. The humming seems to change from an even-sounding noise to an eerie rising and falling whistle. You think you know what it is. An electric motor is stuck somewhere beneath the floor; you've heard sounds like that when your father was working on a faulty electric motor in his garage shop. You relax—nothing strange about it—and start forward once more.

But suddenly the whistling sound changes to an ear-piercing whine. You smell something. It has to be smoke, for when you look down through the dim light you see cloudy vapors rise from cracks in the wood.

You scream. There's a fire beneath you!

You spin about, intending to run outside. But the mirrors are all around you, and you can't be sure which direction to run!

Turn to page 11.

That's the craziest thing you've heard! It's just an amusement park ride, isn't it? And it'll have to stop sooner or later. Even if this creature is laughing at you, is making fun of you—that's just part of the "fun" of being here.

You think. You hope.

But just as you reach the very top again, when you think if you just relax and hold still you'll be able to ride safely to the end, the troll stands up. And even though it's not any taller than you, its shoulders are very, very broad. Its other arm swings about, a second claw-fingered hand grabs your other wrist, and before you can do more than let out a wild scream, the thing lifts you from the spinning chair, holds you aloft a moment, then flings you out!

Toward the Gulf of Mexico? Turn to page 52.
Or toward another of the wild rides? Turn to page 23.

40

You don't know what these heads are—maybe they once were part of people, with the bodies hidden by the boxlike pedestals they seem to sit on. But whatever they are, you don't want to take any chances.

You make yourself seem to relax; that'll catch them off guard. You glance slowly from one to the other. When they seem to be quiet, when their shrieks are little more than wordless sounds, you set yourself, then suddenly charge toward the door.

At once, they start screaming again: *"Catch the kid! Catch the kid! Catch all kids—tonight!"*

You force yourself to disregard their cries and lower your shoulder just as you reach the door. You slam hard into it and bounce backward so quickly you fall to the floor.

The heads scream even louder, this time without words. The room becomes filled with the din. And when you look frantically from one to another, you notice something else—the pedestals all begin to move . . .

Toward you!

Turn to page 54.

For one brief moment, then, you're perfectly still. You hope the machine will *not* work as it's supposed to. You hope, instead, that it has brakes and will descend very slowly.

But it does not!

At first, it vibrates. Then you hear three rapid clicks, and with a swish of air you start falling—straight down!

You squeeze your eyes tightly shut, bracing your feet for the sudden stop that *has* to break your fall. Your stomach rises until you *know* it's stuck in your throat. Your breath leaves you and you feel a horrible prickling sensation along your spine.

Faster . . . faster . . . faster you fall!

You try to scream, but there's no air in your lungs. You grab at the edge of the seat with one hand, try to clutch the back with the other. But you're bouncing so hard you can't hold on. You grab the safety bar and squeeze it. But you pull so hard you bend it, pinning yourself in the chair. That's all right, you tell yourself, the attendant can release you when the chair stops.

Metal clangs against metal, something grinds hard against the rails, and you think you know what's happened, the braking system has failed! Oh, no!

But does it stop safely anyhow? Turn to page 20.

42

"You want to go? You want to leave Riptide Wonders?"

"I sure do," you say. "It's . . . it's not what I thought!"

"But *nobody* ever wants to leave Riptide."

The way this clown says it, you're beginning to wonder if he will take you somewhere you don't want to go.

He begins to lead you away from the building. "We don't like for *anybody* to leave," he says.

You swallow hard. "I . . . I'll come back another time." You're not sure—once you get away—if you'll ever come back. But you *might*—that's the truth.

He gives your arm a shake and you're now certain he is going to carry you someplace you don't want to go. But then he stops, squats down, looks at you, and laughs real loud. "All right, kid." He fumbles in his huge pocket and brings out a blue card with red printing on it. "And when you come back, this ticket will give you a free chance to take three rides. Just tell the people at the gate Laughing Johnny's your friend!"

Laughing Johnny, you think as you walk toward the gate. *Laughing Johnny,* you mutter as you cross the road to wait on a bus that will take you back to the motel. Laughing Johnny nearly scared you to death.

Well, *thank you very much, Laughing Johnny!* But I don't think I'll ever want to come back to Riptide Wonders. Not ever . . .

THE END

For though they vaguely remind you of walruses and sea lions, vicious moray eels and poisonous sting-rays—one even looks like a cross between a flying fish and a huge leather-winged bird—they all make you think of creatures that existed millions of years ago and lived with equal ease on land or in the water.

43

But why are these things in this amusement park?

You do not have time to wonder. Before you can turn to flee, the witch cackles, "Something to play with, my pretties!"

You shake all over. "Get me out of here—"

But the witch suddenly vanishes in a puff of red fire.

The fire puts the creatures into a frenzy of motion and terrifying noises. They begin advancing toward you, some moving on little finlike flippers, some slithering like snakes, some flapping about like fish out of water, and the big bird waddles!

The noises they make are grunts, coughlike growls, and ear-piercing whistles. You back toward the hall-way, but discover that a door has closed it off. You cannot open it!

As the creatures close about you, you kick at them, swing your arms, scream for them to leave you alone. But a moray eel bites you, a stingray stings you, and the leather-winged fish-bird knocks you to the floor.

And you know . . . as the rest swarm over you . . . that you will never . . . leave this . . . weird . . . amusement . . . park . . .

THE END

44

The very idea makes you break out in a cold sweat. Quicksand!

You think that's what you've stepped into.

You try to turn, but one foot sinks down until the gooey sand is up to your ankle. You shift madly once more, and the other foot also sinks down!

You flail your arms, reaching for the smoother, harder floor, but it's just beyond your fingertips!

You slowly sink down to your knees, down to your hips, down to your waist.

You squirm, you twist, you grunt and wiggle. You try with all your might to lay yourself out flat, thinking that will keep you from going down.

But nothing works.

You scream. But all you hear as an answer are the echoing cries from the room of talking heads: *"Catch all kids—catch all kids!—Tonight we catch all kids!"*

You sink to your stomach, to your chest, to your shoulders, to your neck. Your arms swing and stretch, shift and struggle. But they, too, are soon sucked into the gooey muck.

You scream one last time, just before your mouth and nose and eyes and ears are clogged with quicksand.

And your last—thought—is—nobody . . . ought . . . to . . . have . . . quicksand . . . in . . . an . . . amusement . . . park . . .

THE END

As the force of the explosion weakens, you begin to descend. You scream again and again—and you cover your face with your hands.

45

Dumb, dumb, dumb. You should have stayed with Mrs. Howe, gone to the movies, stayed at the motel to watch TV reruns, anything but this!

Finally, when you know it's only a matter of seconds until you hit something, you force yourself to open your eyes, and you don't believe it! You're heading into somebody's beach game volleyball net.

You slam into it, the supporting poles bend over, the net breaks your fall, and you tumble safely onto piles of loose sand.

You don't care if sand gets in your shoes. You don't care if it gets in your ears and nose and mouth! All you care about is getting up, brushing yourself off, dog-trotting to the bus stop, and returning to the motel!

Maybe someday you'll go to another amusement park—maybe.

THE END

46

It's real—*it's horribly, horribly real!*

But as it wriggles and squirms and slowly wraps itself around you, you realize one thing—it is *not* an octopus tentacle. You think of a snake, but this terrifying creature is no ordinary snake.

Your thoughts race frantically—you shudder all over when you realize what it is.

It's an electric eel, a long, thick-bodied, snakelike, slimy electric eel. And you know from something you once read in a book about creatures of the deep that an electric eel can produce enough volts to shock a horse!

That would be enough to kill . . .

You tremble at the thought.

Forgetting the mirrors, you twist about, grabbing with both hands at this cold, slippery creature. You clutch it, only to have your fingers slide off. You grab again, but before you can do more than touch it once more, the thing wriggles about and seems to glide about your hips.

You try to run but the thing is so long that part of it wraps itself around your legs. You fall, and suddenly you're in water!

You're not supposed to be anywhere near water! But you are. As you roll and twist, trying to escape this deep-sea creature, you sense waves rising and washing over you!

Turn to page 59.

48

Your heart is pounding as hard as if you'd just run two hundred yards uphill. You know that any minute the operator down on the ground will press a button or turn some kind of wheel and you'll go flying down—straight down.

You clench your teeth. You squeeze the safety bar so hard your knuckles turn white. And you're ready . . .

. . . But not for what *really* happens!

For at that moment the whole tower begins to tremble. You think it's an earthquake, the shaking gets so terrible. Then it begins to rock from side to side, first leaning toward the Gulf of Mexico, then whipping back the other way.

You wrap your arms about the safety bar; you turn your feet so that you can dig your heels into the footrest. And you tilt your head back, trying to press it against the back of the seat.

The tower starts rocking in the opposite direction—and then you hear an explosive *crack!*

The tower has broken off its huge concrete base!

Turn to page 117.

Your feet slip and lose their hold on the support arm. You cling tightly, trying not to fall into the water, and look down. And you see why the pole stopped falling. There, standing on the Pier Flipper's track, his legs braced against the still clattering engine, is the giant figure you saw in the amusement park's midway. The gleaming silver garb seems to ripple, as if heavy muscles beneath it were extending themselves.

You try to stop yourself, for now you know you're slipping off the padded vehicle arm. But your fingers just aren't strong enough and they lose their grip.

You fall—but not far. Before you can drop into the water, the giant grabs you and swings you about. You're glad not to fall into the Gulf but you're not so sure about this creature holding you.

You hope he'll just walk the rails to shore, put you down, then come back to see about the engine. He does carry you to shore—but he does not put you down. Holding you aloft as if you were some kind of prize animal, he carries you down the midway, saying not a word.

When you're safely away from the Pier Flipper, you try to catch his attention. "I can walk."

He does not respond. His fingers, however, seem to grasp you more firmly.

Will he carry you to another of the park's rides? Turn to page 25.
Or does this frightening giant have other ideas? Turn to page 56.

50

You're just inside the *one* walk-through house you had no desire to enter: the Swamp Jungle. You know there'll be huge lizards, deadly snakes, alligators, jungle cats, perhaps some crocodiles. You're not sure what the difference is between crocodiles and alligators, but you know you don't want to confront either.

You ease yourself out of the box and step onto the floor. You'd rather go right back out but you are worried that the giant might be waiting. It's best to go to the far end, if you can get there.

You walk cautiously, looking sharply right and left. You make up your mind that if any animal moves, you'll stop in your tracks, you will not disturb it.

Strangely, however, you don't see anything moving. As you go past swamp and jungle displays, you gradually relax; the place has pictures instead of real animals. Pictures and plants, although the plants seem to be real.

You come to a turn, hesitate, then glance quickly to your left. Something is moving in the underbrush!

You stare, but whatever it is, it's keeping itself out of sight. You stand still a moment longer, then you start forward once more.

It is then that you become conscious of a peculiar odor.

It's like some kind of perfumed gas, and as you breathe more of it, you feel your stomach muscles begin to tighten.

Turn to page 118.

51

You glance from one to the other, then decide the saddlelike seat on the squid is too small, so you choose the turtle. You move toward it and pull yourself up onto it. You shift about and make yourself comfortable. You catch the reins in one hand, let your other hand fall lightly on the pole, then you glance toward the man at the controls. Within seconds, you hear the heavy motor begin to whir and the merry-go-round slowly starts to move.

The turtle quivers a couple of times, then it starts to rise and fall, rise and fall—just as it's supposed to do.

But the merry-go-round seems pretty tame; it's too slow. And for a moment you halfway wish you'd gone to the House of Mirrors instead.

But within seconds, the thing starts moving more rapidly. You clutch the pole more tightly and wrap your fingers about the reins.

Now the machine is *really* whirling. The faces of people standing around form one rapid, colorful blur. Even their bodies appear to stretch as you move faster and faster!

You begin to notice something else that you hadn't expected: the turtle's head begins to move right and left, right and left. And its mighty jaws start to open and close!

Turn to page 72.

52

In the glare of the lights you can't be sure which way you're falling, but when you look down, you think you're going toward the shoreline. No! You're going farther out: you're going into the water!

You can swim, but at night there might be a strong undertow, and you can't swim against that.

But at the last minute, when you look again, you see something like a narrow walkway that goes out over the water. And you remember the folder describing Riptide Wonders. There's a strange ride called the Pier Flipper that goes out over the water. The walkway has two train-track rails, and a powerful motor rolls over it. Attached to both sides of the motor and sticking out over the water are huge wagon-wheel-like devices, except that they have no rims. Instead, at the end of the wheels' spokes are small seats; the whole thing looks like two small ferris wheels. As the motor rolls along the tracks, those wheels turn and the riders go up, then down, almost into the water.

When the tide's in they probably get wet!

You take a breath just before you splash into the Gulf! And the minute you're in the water, you begin kicking and pumping your arms, trying to surface. You're wondering if you'll ever make it—when your right arm strikes something.

A shark or dolphin? Or something man-made? Turn to page 5.

53

You look from one head to another, and as you do so, you suddenly realize that they remind you of pictures you've seen in history books and encyclopedias. One looks like the famous British murderer Jack the Ripper, another looks like Dracula, a third looks like the monster Frankenstein, a fourth looks like Bluebeard, and one of them looks like that pirate, that Captain Hook. The one that looks half ape, half man reminds you of some prehistoric creature.

But whatever they look like, they're frightening.

One thing you cannot afford to do, however: you *cannot* let your fear keep you from rescuing yourself.

You're not sure whether these things can make their boxlike pedestals move, but you sure hope not. Just to make certain they can't catch you in case they're able to move, you take three cautious steps toward the door through which you entered. That'll get their attention; then you can switch and dart through the other door before they can stop you.

If you make it through that door, turn to page 62.
If you fail to make it through, turn to page 40.

54

The boxes can't be made of cardboard or some other light substance. For as they start to close in, the floor begins to vibrate. Those things can hammer you to death!

The thought horrifies you. You look wildly about, seeking an avenue of escape. And you notice one thing: the ape-man head is the only one that does *not* move! It remains beside the door, as if it is going to guard against your running that way again.

Riptide Wonders! What kind of amusement park is it? Nobody is supposed to get hurt—maybe scared, but not hurt! But you can't take time to think about that. You've got to get out of here.

You glance toward the room's ceiling and you make a startling discovery. It's not very high. It's really not a solid roof at all but part of a tent, and it's sagging. If there's just some way to leap . . .

Hey, that's it! You know you can move faster than these boxlike things! You'll just run hard into one of them, knock a head off, leap onto the pedestal, and jump up to the canvas. It has three large air holes in it. All you'll have to do is grab one of those, swing up, and rip your way free!

You look about furtively, select the head that looks like Captain Hook, and suddenly spring toward it.

Does it fall off the pedestal? Turn to page 8.
Or does the pedestal have a surprise for you? Turn to
page 71.

You want to reach up for the canvas, but first you must be sure of your balance. You slowly squat down, trying to steady yourself.

55

But just as you think you've gotten the pedestal to be still, the top of it suddenly opens, and a wide, swirling steel band twists upward like a gigantic corkscrew. Before you can do more than stand straight up, the band begins to wind itself about you.

First, it encircles your legs so that you cannot take even a half-inch step. Then it works upward, encircling your hips, your waist, your chest, your shoulders and arms, not stopping until your entire body from the neck down is totally controlled.

You scream and try to twist free, but you cannot.

Then slowly, very slowly, it begins to draw you downward and into the body of the pedestal. Within seconds, even while you yell and holler, it completely encloses you within the heavy pedestal—completely, that is, except for your head and part of your neck.

You try to kick inside the container. But you cannot. You struggle to free your arms, without success.

And in that terrifying moment you understand . . .

You will not escape. For now *you* are one of them. *You* are . . . part . . . of . . . the . . . amusement park . . . you . . . are . . . a . . . talking head . . .

THE END

56

Frantically, you look about, hoping some of the people enjoying the concessions or merely walking from one of the rides to another will look up. Not one glances your way.

When you see that they don't seem to care, you yell at the giant, "Put me down! I said, *put me down!*"

He does not look at you. He does not laugh. He does not say a word. Instead, he continues carrying you aloft until he comes to a narrow alleylike path running between a hot dog and cold drink stand and a large storage trailer. There, he stops beside a huge lockerlike box, lifts the lid, and plops you inside. "Bad kid, stay here!" And before you can yell at him to let you alone, he clamps the lid down on you.

In the dark you don't know what else is inside. But you're not going to wait to find out. You give him a couple of minutes to go away, then you test the top. It's not locked!

You start to push it open—but just as you do, you feel the whole thing begin to move.

Turn to page 34.

57

You yell and kick your legs and wildly swing your arms about, but there's nothing to keep you from flying through the air.

You fly well above the amusement park, almost as high as the Drop-Off tower, then you begin to fall. You're sure you'll break all your bones when you hit the ground . . .

But for some lucky reason, you don't fall all the way down. As luck would have it, you descend over the Ski Glide, a kind of hang glider that goes around and around, up and down, on a long arm. When you land, you find yourself in the seat of one of the hang gliders.

You grab on to the passenger safety bar, quickly latch it in place, and look down. You were lucky! If you'd fallen another twenty feet, you'd have landed solidly on a concrete walkway!

But now you're riding.

The hang glider dips and soars, dips and soars, and as it moves in the controlled circle, it seems to go faster and faster.

At first, it's a good feeling, and you remember that earlier you'd planned to ride it, anyway.

But as it picks up speed, you begin to wonder about it. These things are supposed to give you the feeling that you're actually riding out over a lake or the ocean, but this is too real!

Turn to page 78.

58

When it's your time to climb aboard, you impulsively select the squid, since it's so very different looking. You glance at the odd reins that are fastened to its mouth, then you slip onto the saddle. As your legs slip down along the sides, you sense something very peculiar. This thing isn't made of wood or plastic. It feels soft and cold and—slimy?

But you tell yourself that's part of the fun of this park.

The music starts, the machine starts moving the merry-go-round, and within seconds the squid is going up and down, up and down.

It also seems to be doing something else, something you had *not* expected. Those long feelers or legs, or whatever they are, keep moving about and you have a hard time remaining on the saddle.

It slips once and you think you're going to fall off. You grab on to the upright pole and slide back into position. For a moment you have the weird feeling that you're not on a real merry-go-round, that you're riding some sea creature that's not attached to anything!

Turn to page 77.

59

You do not understand it but somehow, as you struggled with this horrid *thing*, you escaped from the House of Mirrors. Perhaps you stumbled through a door, or maybe you fell through the floor. You do not know.

And you do not care. All you want is for this electric eel to leave you alone!

But it does not. Instead, it seems to be drawing itself tighter and tighter around your body.

Then suddenly something slams itself against your chest, something like a rubber-headed hammer, and instantly you feel tingling, burning shocks pass through your body.

You're instantly stunned.

The creature's blunted head strikes you again and again and again. Powerful volts of electricity pass through your body, and you sense sparks flashing in all directions.

You scream. You try to twist and turn. But you cannot free yourself.

And as you slowly lose consciousness your last thought is that an amusement park should not be allowed to house electric eels . . .

THE END

60

You've just been delivered to the storage room of either the horror house or the most frightening art museum you've ever heard of.

You raise the box lid a few inches, then you stop and listen. Nothing, nothing except the noise from the midway and all the rides coming through the wall of the room.

Cautiously, you raise the lid higher and ease yourself out of the box and onto a dirty, poorly carpeted floor. You stand for a moment, one hand resting on the box, and stare about.

The light is dim yellow, with occasional flashes of red, orange, purple, and green. As the colored flashes beam and glow about the room, you see all sorts of horrible-looking heads, each one fixed atop round boxes that stand three to four feet off the floor. Some of the heads have thick hair, some are bald with long beards, some have grotesque features, and all are various shades of brown. As you peer closely, three have blood, or something that looks like blood, oozing from what appear to be knife slashes along their necks.

Turn to page 68.

62

You prepare yourself, take three steps toward the big door, then you stop, suddenly whirl about, and dash as hard and fast as you can toward the smaller one. You get through the little aisle separating five of those heads on the right side from the six or seven on the other. You sidestep and dart past the ape-man head. And with all the strength you can muster, you bang into the door.

"Catch the kid! Catch the kid! *Catch all kids!*" The cry echoes through the room, shrill voices mingling with deeper ones.

But that does not stop you. And when your shoulder strikes the door, it breaks from its old hinges and falls onto the floor.

You fall on top of it but hastily scramble to your feet. The floor is hard, bare wood, you guess, and you're glad of that. It'll be easier to run on . . .

. . . Except that the hard surface runs out very quickly!

You pass beyond the broken door, take three steps—and all of a sudden discover something soft and very, very mushy. You start to sink.

You sniff hard, and the odor makes you think of some dismal swamp, creatures that dwell in swamps, and something else—something called *quicksand!*

Turn to page 44.

But you're caught by the waistband of your jeans and held dangling over the midway. But even though you're no longer falling, you're sure your jeans will rip and you'll plunge to earth!

Wildly you look down at the crowd. The people are pointing up and shouting, but not one of them tries to help.

You hear cloth tear. Again you yell, and this time the clown dashes from the souvenir stand, his baggy shirt and britches flapping in the breeze. He stops right beneath you, looks up, then suddenly takes off his belt. He grabs the waistband of his britches and spreads them way out.

Dumb, dumb, dumb—but before you can finish the thought, your jeans suddenly tear away! You are falling again, toward the paved midway! The clown totters right and left, back and forth, as if trying to get right under you.

Just as you're about to splatter on the pavement, he moves right—and you fall into the cushiony softness of those ballooning clown britches!

Laughing as if it's part of an act, the clown lifts you out and puts you down. You swallow hard, spin about, and dash toward the park entrance. You know you ought to thank the clown; after all, he saved your life. But you'll come back tomorrow to do that. Right now all you want to do is get away from Riptide Wonders, far, far away . . .

THE END

64

This huge mechanical turtle begins to run like a live animal straight towad the water's edge!

You've read about giant sea turtles, that they can swim out as far as they want to. They can swim all the way to an island if that's their home. And this one, whatever else it is, seems to be heading toward some distant place!

You try to get off. You swing your foot over, but before you can put it on the ground, this horrid beast raises its ugly head, its wicked mouth opens, and it clamps down on your ankle!

You scream and try to pull away. But it's too strong. You cannot free yourself.

You look frantically this way and that. You know Riptide Wonders is supposed to be a fun place, a nice amusement park. But something is terribly wrong!

The creature reaches a low embankment and half slides, half crawls down it, and takes you within ten feet of the water's edge.

You're about to enter and you know you cannot free your ankle from those massive jaws when you hear a powerful shout. You glance back, and see the broad-shouldered midget dashing over the low sand dunes, heading in your direction and waving his arms.

He's coming to help. But does he make it in time? Turn to page 89.

Or, once he reaches you, does he really help? Turn to page 82.

63

66

You don't know what's going on or what's about to happen—but you do know one thing: you're not going to wait to find out!

Just before the flying shrunken head strikes you, you duck hard and drop to your knees. Without looking back, you begin to crawl as fast as you can toward the crack. And as you get closer, you realize that, sure enough, there's a side door—perhaps one used by the people who take care of this House of Horrors.

You reach the door, you half raise yourself, and you grab for the knob. But just as your fingers are about to turn it, you feel something stick into your leg.

You whirl about and you discover to your horror that the little round head that was walking moments ago is now settled against you—and chewing your flesh!

You scream and try to slap it away.

As you do, the shrunken head descends quickly and bangs against your shoulder, knocking you flat.

Before you can move again, all the shrunken heads drop from the wall and fly at you.

Turn to page 84.

When you reach the House of Horrors, however, the entrance is blocked off, as if the place has been closed. That does not stop the midget. He kicks the barrier aside, carries you through the curtained-off doorway, and dumps you on the floor. And as he leaves, he grabs the heavy door and slams it shut, sending the curtain flying off.

For a moment you sit there, stunned. This is *not* one of the attractions you'd intended visiting. You look around, seeking a possible exit, since you assume the main door's locked. You think you spot a small crack to your left, probably a side door for people who work at the amusement park. You get to your feet and slowly start toward the crack. But the room is so dimly lighted that you don't see any of the exhibits.

You move slowly, trying to make sure you don't bump into anything. But just as you think you're close to the exit, you step on something round and solid. All at once, beams of blue, orange, and green lights flood the room.

You stop abruptly and stare about. And what you see terrifies you. To your right, you see what looks like a body cut into three pieces—a lower half, the torso, and the head. The pieces are lying on what appears to be a blood-soaked sheet. Just beyond it, held up by long hair knotted and hooked against a board support, is the bearded head of a one-eyed pirate. And lying on the floor beneath it is a long, blood-stained dagger.

House of Horrors is right! Turn to page 80.

68

Very cautiously, you move nearer the closest one. Its face is lined with wrinkles, its eyes are deeply set, and its mouth is half open, showing jagged teeth. You hesitate a moment, then you gingerly stretch forth your hand.

Just as the tip of your finger touches its cheek, you hear a dreadful shriek—from the head you just touched.

You jump back.

At once, a second shriek joins the first, and within seconds four or five others join in the chorus.

You clap your hands over your ears, the din is so frightening.

Then a deep voice, rumbling like a distant drum, speaks through the din of shrieks: *"All kids must die!"*

You jerk your hand away from your ears, startled by the voice, and spin about. In the room's far corner, on a pedestal that's taller than the others, is the giant head of something that looks half ape, half man. Its mouth is much larger than any of the others, and its pointed ears are wide-set.

When you stare at it, the face contorts with rage: *"Catch the kid! Catch the kid!"*

If you decide to run out, turn to page 12.
But if you choose to get back in the box, turn to page 32.

You grab hold, then you keep low until it has settled. As soon as it is still, you gingerly stand, and just as you hoped, you can reach the canvas holes. You extend your hands through two of them and discover, luckily, a rope that is used to keep the canvas from falling. You grab it with both hands and carefully pull yourself up. One of the holes is quite small, but the other is large enough for you to work yourself through.

Within a couple of minutes you're out of the talking head room and are precariously balanced on the flopping canvas top. Using the rope to guide yourself, you work your way to the edge of the building and climb down the outer wall. For a moment, you are in semidarkness, hidden from the midway's lights by the small building. You glance right and left, then step out . . .

And bump hard into one of the figures you'd seen earlier, the clown. He bends over—you think it's a "he"—and pokes his big round nose right into your face. And suddenly both his cheeks light up as if from bulbs inside his jaws.

You leap backward.

The clown laughs and grabs your arm. His fingers are much, much too strong; you cannot break free. You look into his eyes—you think they're real eyes—and your mouth begins to quiver. "I . . . I just want to go," you say.

Turn to page 42.

70

And now you're spinning much, much too fast! Other riders begin to holler and scream. You glance frantically toward the center of the merry-go-round. The operator has fallen down and his leg is caught in the huge control belt—he can't do anything to stop the mad whirling!

You see one of the dolphins go flying off the track, carrying a young boy with it. A pole on the opposite side breaks, and the stingray a girl is riding bounces off the track and falls under the merry-go-round's platform.

While your attention is diverted, the squid's shell-like body seems to swell. The saddle begins to slip to the side.

You scream, but before the sound is fully out of your throat another tentacle creeps beneath your shirt and slides up your back. It comes to your neck, then slowly the thing encircles . . .

When it is completely around your neck, the suction-cup end attaches itself to you.

You grab for it. It's getting tighter and tighter. Your finger touches it, and you *know* it's not mere padded plastic. It's got the live feel of a creature from the deep.

You try to struggle with the tentacle, but you cannot free yourself. And even as you clutch at the one around your neck, others seem to come crawling up your body, wrapping themselves around your waist, your chest, your thighs . . .

Turn to page 86.

You take three steps, then you jump up and swing both hands as hard as you can. The head, which feels very much like a real, live one, totters right and left. A horrid groan comes from its wide lips, and it totters off the pedestal. You leap again and this time you land on top of the stand.

The trouble is, you hadn't thought about any mechanism being inside it. The minute your feet touch the top, you somehow step on a triggerlike device. The surface breaks loose, a mighty spring inside the pedestal is released, and before you can do anything to stop yourself, you are sprung violently upward. You tear through the canvas top and are terrified to find that you are being thrown straight up, far too fast and too hard!

Turn to page 57.

72

The people who designed this ride surely made it realistic!

But before you can think much about the merry-go-round's designers, you begin to wonder if you're not going too fast. For the blurring seems more frightening, and the wind is blowing your hair more than it should.

The turtle is jostling you too hard, much too hard.

You turn toward the machine operator, hoping he will decide to slow the thing down, but he's merely laughing at the riders!

Now the turtle is bouncing more violently than ever.

Just when you're sure, though, that it cannot possibly bounce off the machine, the pole holding it in place breaks—and all at once the turtle is flung off the machine!

You yell and hope that it will land in a pile of straw or loose sand. But it does neither. It falls on a huge patch of sparce grass—and the weirdest of all things happens . . .

Turn to page 64.

You don't know what's going on, but one thing you're quite certain of: you have no intention of remaining in this crazy House of Horrors. Perhaps the main entrance is closed off, though you can think of no good reason why it should be. But no matter—you're getting out!

You set yourself, glance back once, fix your attention on what has to be a side door, and then you spring forward and charge toward it.

Instantly, all the heads scream at once and the noise they make is terrifying. But you do not stop. You slam hard into the wall area you think is a door.

It is not a door; rather, it's some kind of curtain made to resemble a doorway. But no matter—the curtain gives and you tumble forward . . .

And bang solidly into—*somebody?*

You bounce against something that feels human and fall back onto a very soft floor. You scramble to your feet at once and look up into the very angry face of that huge, silvery-costumed giant you saw in the midway.

Turn to page 90.

74

For a moment you're stunned, but after a minute or so you're able to look up. The giant is towering over you, his gloved hands on his hips. Those orange eyes are staring down at you and the masked face seems more ominous than ever. Although he does not say a word, you're sure he means to hurt you.

Pretending to relax, you roll over on your side, moving very slowly. And once your gaze shifts from that awful face, you glance hastily right and left, looking for an avenue of escape. Your captor is huge, but you're much lower now than you were before, and you think you can spin about, get to your feet, and scramble out of here before he can bend over to grab you.

But just as you set yourself to spring away from him, he slips a huge foot underneath you, and before you can make another move, that foot lifts you straight up!

Again those powerful gloved hands close, but this time they're clapped about your head.

Turn to page 83.

Golvan raises his foot again and you think he's about to shove you once more. Instead, he puts the huge foot right on your stomach and presses down!

The pain is terrible and you want to cry out, but you don't have enough air in your lungs to make a sound. He bends forward, foot still pushing, and stares down at you. "Right size, right shape."

You frown. Right size and right shape—for what?

You don't know, but right now you've got to get your breath. You catch his heavy foot with both hands and shove as hard as you can. He resists for a moment, then gradually lets you push it. When you're free, you half roll on your side. And you *know* one thing. You've got to get away. There's no telling what he'll do with you.

You stay still for a moment, breathing hard. Then you turn over, get to your knees, and start crawling. You know he's still staring down at you but for some reason he does not try to stop you immediately. And in that brief moment, you think perhaps he's letting you escape.

But the hope is short-lived.

For just as you think you can get away, he hollers, stomps his huge foot, shaking the building, and lunges forward. And this time he does not kick. He bends over and grabs you about the neck. He picks you up as if you were a tiny kitten . . .

Turn to page 115.

76

Not only are you in one of the seats—you're in the very front car. The attendant is so busy he doesn't notice that you don't have a ticket. He fastens you in, then turns to the next rider.

At that moment something weird and wrong and terrible happens. The car you're sitting in starts to move!

You look around and see the attendant hollering at somebody messing with the controls! A midget!

You hear metal clicking against metal. Desperately, you grab the restraining bar and glance over your shoulder. It's worse than you thought. The car you're in has been disconnected from the other six, and you're moving all by yourself.

You do not want to ride this thing! And you *really* don't want to ride it all by yourself!

Turn to page 79.

The merry-go-round motor seems to speed up, and you're going faster and faster! As you accelerate, the squid's long feelers bounce up and down, up and down. And you can't help feeling that something you had not expected is about to happen.

One of those long tentacles suddenly wraps itself around your right leg. You try to kick it off. But for some reason it seems to stick to your bare skin, just above the ankle. And it's terribly cold!

You kick out, hoping to free your legs. But just then the merry-go-round begins to jerk forward, stutter, then jerk forward again. You're lurching, and your hand slips from the guide pole. You reach wildly for the reins, but instead of catching leather your fingers close over one of the squid's bouncing tentacles.

Immediately, you feel the little suction thing at the tentacle end latch on to your palm. You try to jerk free, but you cannot.

Turn to page 70.

78

Faster and faster you spin. When you first landed on it, you were able to look down and make out people. But now, with the increased speed, the people, the lights, and even the midway all turn into a rainbow-colored blur, like an unfocused TV screen.

You hear a sudden noise and look to your left. It's the long, polelike arm to which the hang glider is attached. Something is breaking loose!

Oh, no!

But before you can do anything more than grab the retaining safety bar, the hang glider breaks free, and all of a sudden you're sent sailing out . . .

Into the darkness . . .

Out over the Gulf of Mexico.

And you keep going higher and higher, higher and higher.

Within seconds, you're far, far out over the water. When you look back, the amusement park is little more than a blur of lights. You look beyond, toward the highway, and all you can see is a thin line of automobile lights.

You swallow hard, you shake the safety bar, and you kick your feet. Somehow, you've got to turn this thing around!

But you cannot . . . you keep sailing out over the Gulf . . . and within minutes, you're out of sight of land . . . and you wonder if you will sail all the way to South America . . . or if you'll slowly descend into the rolling, storm-tossed waves . . .

THE END

Again the attendant hollers at the midget. The midget screams back at him. The attendant dashes for the controls, but the midget grabs a lever, jerks it all the way back, then breaks it off and throws it at the attendant. It misses and sails past him, slamming into a huge metal box. At once, sparks fly, the lights along the roller coaster go out, and you're all alone in a car that's just reaching the high point of the track. From there on, it'll pick up speed!

The car reaches the peak, creaks, moves forward slowly—then begins to rush down the first main slope. It goes faster and faster, and you have to turn your head, the wind is so strong! You come to the first rise. The car charges up it, banks right—and you're in the first loop of the corkscrew turn. You counted those loops when you first looked at the Mad Dog—there are four—and they turn you upside down, every one of them!

You go faster and faster, yelling all the while for somebody to help you. As you rocket into the third loop, you look frantically back toward the control area. You see men gathering around the remaining cars, shoving them onto a small siding. And you think you know what that means . . .

Turn to page 108.

80

The blood on the dagger seems fresh!

You slowly turn and stare all around you. You see the skeleton of a huge man, held erect by a steel pole, a smoking pipe stuck between its fleshless jaws. Across from it is another skeleton, this one of a huge sea creature; you can't be sure whether it's a shark or whale. Just on the other side of it, you see a row of shrunken heads, all dangling by strands of black, thick hair. When you glance to your right, you see what appears to be a half-human, half-fish object, the upper half reminding you of a vicious, bearded pirate, the lower half looking much like the body and fins of a hammerhead shark.

You shudder all over. You did *not* want to come here.

You hear a slight noise and quickly look to your left. What you see makes you gasp. Coming slowly toward you is the round, grotesque head of an old woman. The thing has no body, but short legs seem to grow down from the neck. And little bare feet move slowly over the dirty floor.

Why did that midget save you just to bring you here?

You do not know, but one thing's for sure, you don't intend to stay!

You quickly shift your gaze toward the main entrance, from it to the crack you'd seen earlier, and from the crack to the ceiling. There has to be a way out . . .

Turn to page 88.

82

The midget doesn't stop until he dashes past you and gets around the turtle. He stops inches from the water's edge, whirls about, and drops to the sandy shore. Rolling on his back, he lets the turtle ride up and almost on top of him, then he grabs its front feet and gives them a violent jerk and twist.

The object's huge mouth opens as the head tries to turn toward the attacker, and in that instant you pull free. The moment your ankle is released, you twist away and roll to the left. You hit the sand and keep rolling. You want to get far away from that *thing!*

As soon as he sees you're off, the midget kicks hard, slides out from under the turtle and hops to his feet. But he is *not* laughing. His wrinkled face is twisted with anger. "Dumb kid!" he yells. And before you can move another inch, he grabs you around the waist and swings you up onto his shoulder.

And they're muscle-hard!

Without another word, he carries you back toward the amusement park midway. When you're past the still-whirling merry-go-round, you tap his arm. "I can walk," you say.

"Shut up!" he hisses back.

And he continues carrying you toward the entrance to the House of Horrors!

Turn to page 67.

The giant laughs. You're held so close to him that his fire-hot breath seems to burn your cheeks and hair. "In Golvan's power!" he roars.

You wiggle and writhe, but you're little more than a dangling mouse in his grasp. You look anxiously about, wondering what this room is, and in the low light you see forms. Forms? No, they're more than mere forms, they're statues. You see one that looks like a soldier, another that looks like a cowboy. And as your frantic gaze sweeps the room, you see what appear to be statues of famous people. There's a man in an astronaut's suit, somebody that looks like George Washington, a figure that reminds you of John Wayne, and a double statue that reminds you of those infamous outlaws Bonnie and Clyde.

You see three others, little statues, that do not belong with the big ones.

Statues of children.

As the giant carries you past them, you suddenly realize where the terrible smell comes from. It's from freshly poured wax.

A chilling tremble passes through you. For you suddenly *know* what the giant who calls himself Golvan has in store for you.

What? Turn to page 98.

84

You roll on your side, flailing your arms and kicking at the round, chewing head. Your right hand strikes a shrunken one, and immediately it begins to scream.

You don't like it. You don't like it at all! You came to this amusement park to have fun, but this is no fun—*no fun at all!*

You kick once, this time catching "round head" solidly. Before it can recover, you leap to your feet, charge the side door, and bang against it. And luck is with you—

It flies open!

You do not look back. Ignoring all the people who stare at you, you make a mad dash for the park entrance. You'll cross the street, you'll find where the bus stops. You'll catch it—and return to the motel.

You hate watching TV reruns—but you'd rather do that than stay in this place and get eaten by bodyless heads in some spooky House of Horrors . . .

THE END

You stop short, suddenly frightened. Boats—there ought to be little boats floating in this shallow stream. And people—the people should be shouting or laughing. But you don't see any boats or hear anyone. Wait a minute . . . when you first entered Riptide Wonders there was a sign at the gate, something about the Tunnel of Love. What was it?

You don't remember, didn't pay much attention to it because you weren't interested.

You take a hesitant step forward. Well, never mind what the sign says, all you want to do is get to the entrance and out of this tunnel—and out of the water.

The shallow water, like a little creek, winds right, then left, then right again. Small overhead lights are too dim to let you see far ahead, but you think you're heading the right way. At least, you hope so.

You walk twenty, maybe twenty-five feet, reach a sharp bend, then suddenly it comes to you. That sign said the Tunnel of Love was closed for . . . for what? Repairs?

That would explain why you don't see boats or hear people. But if they're supposed to be repairing it, why haven't you seen workmen?

You're about to take another step when you hear a loud, swishing noise, like a heavy wave striking rocks.

Are you actually getting close to the Gulf of Mexico? Turn to page 99.

Or does the noise come from some other source? Turn to page 92.

86

You hear a woman scream. Out of the corner of your eye you see the two men dashing down the midway, coming to stop the merry-go-round.

But the tentacles draw tighter.

And you know . . . even as the men . . . come closer . . . that they will . . . not . . . get . . . there . . . in . . . time . . . for you're being choked . . . to . . . death . . . by . . . this . . . giant . . . merry-go-round . . . squid . . .

THE END

You're dazed, and for a moment you cannot focus on anything. But within seconds, your vision adjusts to this stinking room, and you glance around.

You're in the Wax Museum. You'd told yourself earlier that this would be one of the places you meant to see. But you didn't intend to see it this way. You'd expected simply to buy a ticket and enter, just like everybody else.

You look from one statue to another. There's one of John F. Kennedy, another of Abraham Lincoln, one of somebody who's dressed like Superman, and one of a woman who looks like a movie actress, although you can't think of her name. Off near a corner, you spot a statue that resembles King Kong, and on the opposite side of the room there's a giant figure with an axe on its shoulder, like the famous timber man, John Bunyan.

It would have been fun to wander . . .

But before the thought is completed, you feel Golvan's heavy toe digging into your side. He pushes, and you can't help yourself, you roll over.

And that gives you an inspiration! If he does it again, you'll pretend to move just a little; then as soon as the toe relaxes, you'll roll as hard as you can. But toward the entrance.

Does Golvan seem to know what you're thinking? Turn to page 75.

Or does he seem to be enjoying himself so much he's not aware of anything except his pleasure? Turn to page 93.

88

"Yee-ooo-ow!"

The sudden shrill scream almost jerks you around. You stare down at the walking head and discover that it's tilted back so its horrid orange eyes can glare into your face. Light beams are spurting from those eyes.

"Ha-ha-ha, the kid's the right size!"

You stare at the thing, trembling all over. "I'm not supposed to be here."

"Not supposed to be here!"

You spin about. *That* voice came from behind you. You look at the skeleton and discover the bony hand is now holding the pipe, and the fleshless jaw is going up and down.

"But we'll keep you here!"

You swallow hard, lick your lips, turn right and left—there has to be an escape. You hesitate only a moment, then prepare yourself to make a hard dash toward that crack—it *has* to be a door!

But before you can take more than one step, one of those shrunken heads suddenly swings away from the wall, spins in the air, and flies straight at you. The grotesque little mouth keeps opening and shutting, opening and shutting. And each time the lips part, you hear, *"Keep the kid! Keep the kid!"*

Do you run for the door? Turn to page 73.
Or do you fall when you attempt to run? Turn to page 66.

The turtle—you thought it was some kind of made object but now you're not so sure—contin toward the surf, toward those wild, white-capped waves!

You're within five feet of the water when the midget reaches you. He dashes past, whirls about, and kicks hard at the turtle's head. The abrupt move causes the huge creature to stop for a moment. Before it can continue its forward charge, the midget grabs the huge head with both hands.

The turtle shakes violently, but the midget does not release his hold. He kicks once more, shifts right, then grabs the lower jaw.

You didn't think he would be strong enough, but he is, and he finally opens the massive jaws. At once, your leg falls free.

The moment you're released, you spin hard and roll off the seat and onto the sand.

You look at the midget and he's turned the head loose. You yell "Thanks!" and leap to your feet.

You run across the beach toward the amusement park entrance. Never mind all the rides. Never mind the House of Mirrors and the Swamp Jungle—in fact never mind this whole place. You'll find the bus stop and return *right now* to the motel. Mrs. Howe said for you to be back no later than ten o'clock. She won't have to worry. You'll be there, safe, when she and the others return. No more amusement parks for you. At least, not tonight . . .

THE END

90

Before you can make another move, steely-gloved hands grab your shoulders. You're lifted up as if you're nothing more than a limp rag doll. The giant brings you close so that your eyes are only inches from his—except he does not have eyes like most people. You stare into masked eye sockets and see orange-colored eyeballs. Sparks fly from them. You tremble at the sight.

Then the giant's horrible mouth opens and he laughs at you. "*Nobody* breaks into Golvan's house and speaks afterward!"

Trembling all over, you try to nod your head. "I . . . I didn't mean to—"

But he shakes you so hard your tongue starts to waggle in your mouth and you cannot speak another word. "Golvan has places for little ones!"

"I . . . I don't want to go—"

Before you can utter another word, he tucks you firmly under his arm and walks outside. He crosses the midway, ignoring the people who shout at him, and carries you toward a building at the far side of the amusement park. He enters a narrow, dimly lighted passage, turns at the far end and unceremoniously dumps you onto a smelly carpet.

If you think you can escape, turn to page 74.
Or are you fatally trapped? Turn to page 87.

91

Again the witch laughs. But its laughter is abruptly lost in a loud crack as the chain breaks! You feel the chair, the witch, and yourself slung out and away from the whirling machine!

You're sailing over the amusement park, over the beach, and out . . . out . . . out over the rolling waves!

You hear somebody shout below. And within seconds a huge, probing searchlight's beam illuminates you, the chair, and the witch.

Except all of a sudden the witch leaves you, and, spreading its black robe like giant wings, it soars away. It sails up and up, circling like a very small airplane, diving and swooping, rising on the air currents, dipping low, then finally gliding off toward the safety of the beach.

But in the Gravity Whip chair you fly in an arc that first rises—like a ball thrown a great distance—then gradually loses momentum, and begins to fall . . .

Into the turbulent surf.

You scream and yell—but you know your voice cannot be heard above the churning waves!

Turn to page 103.

92

You stand as still as you can, hold your breath, and listen. There, there it is again. And you know it's not waves. Something is there—something is moving ahead of you.

At first you think maybe it's a repairman, but a repairman would have a flashlight, and you see no other lights.

The splashing gets louder.

And with the splashing comes another, more frightening noise. Like something grunting and breathing. It's just around the next bend . . . it's coming closer.

You look back, wondering if there's a way to get back into the House of Mirrors. You're not sure what's approaching, but you don't think you'll like it.

The trouble is, you can't be sure which way to go because the tunnel has a double bend as well as a fork you hadn't noticed before.

The noise suddenly changes. Startled, you spin and stare in its direction. You scream!

Turn to page 105.

You let your arms and legs flop, and Golvan laughs. He puts his hands on his hips, stares down at you, those orange eyes sparking fire, and appears to set his foot to roll you over again.

He's thinking about having more fun with you.

Just as the toe touches your side—and he's balancing himself on the other foot—you spin hard, roll away from the poised toe, spring to your feet, and whirl about. The movement catches the giant by surprise: there he is, toe outstretched and body strained.

Before he can either kick or bend over, you scamper to the left, twist so that even if he grabs for you he cannot catch you, and dash for the passageway you just came through. And this time, once you're through it, you dart right and you find yourself on a narrow path leading to the park's midway.

Not watching which way you go, you run past milling people, between two small snack stands, and onto the roller coaster platform.

Before you can do anything else, you're in one of its wide seats. Suddenly, you're on a ride called the Mad Dog!

Turn to page 76.

94

You hear air hiss from the fun house's small flap-covered entrances. You hear mothers and fathers scream as the whole thing seems to collapse. But you don't care—you're down—and while the air has gone out, creating wrinkles in the surface, you grab on to something. You dig all your fingers into it, try to lie flat, and hope your feet can get caught, too, so that when the fun house expands again, you won't be thrown upward.

And for a brief second, you think you're safe.

But the motor that pumps air into the fun house is too strong to be overcome by your little weight. Within seconds it pumps air back in, and you feel your fingers slipping from the wrinkles. They disappear entirely, and you are flung skyward—much higher than the Triple Spin ride you'd been tossed from.

You don't know how high you are, but while you're caught in the air, about to fall down—certainly to your death—you hear something flap-flap-flap within inches of your head. In a frantic, desperate swing, you glance about . . .

Turn to page 102.

You know the chain is about to break!

Suddenly, this witch creature ceases to laugh. It gently touches your shoulder, and when you look at it, its face is not the horrible thing you first saw. It has turned into that of a kind, smiling old woman. It slips from the chair and grabs onto the chain. It stands, raises its free arm and grasps the side of its flowing costume . . .

And the costume spreads out like a giant parachute.

Before you know it, the Gravity Whip begins to slow down. The rushing wind seems less severe. The chain stops creaking. Within seconds, the whole machine slows down and the swinging chairs drop lower and lower.

A man comes running from the operating machine and looks up at the witch. "Get down! Get down from there!"

Again, the witch's face changes—this time to the long-beaked, wrinkle-cheeked, wide-mouthed creature you first saw. But now its attention is fixed on the man. "I'll eat you for supper!" the creature screams at the man.

The man stops abruptly. He raises both hands, shielding his face. He tries to walk backward but stumbles and falls to the sand-covered walk.

The witch drops nimbly to his side, spreads the cloak, and you can see nothing . . .

Until that creature turns its head and stares at you . . .

Turn to page 110.

96

You don't care what he's hooked. Right now, you don't care what anybody's hooked! All you want to do is get yourself free, out of this giant thing's grasp, and back on the ground. If you do, you know one thing— as soon as your feet hit dirt or sand, you're running— anywhere. You don't care where—

Oh, yes, you do care!

Because the giant creature is about to . . .

He does! He tosses you as far as he can, out over the beach, out near the fishing pier. Well, at least, it'll be in the water . . .

Oh, no! That hammerhead shark!

You fall down and down, arms flailing, legs kicking ready to swim. But when you're within ten feet of the waves, your right arm strikes something like a wire. It jerks, and before you can stop yourself, your arms and legs and body are all entangled in a fishing line. You gulp, because you *know* it's the line belonging to the fisherman holding the pole with the hammerhead shark caught on the baited hook!

The fisherman yells at you: "Stop! Turn it loose!"

You would if you could. But it breaks—somewhere between you and the man. And suddenly you're jerked toward deep water—into the frothing waves . . . out beyond the breakers . . . and you know you've been caught by that hammerhead shark . . .

THE END

For a moment the thing seems to freeze. Then it inhales and lets out a scream right back at you, a scream that's much more shrill than yours was. It's so high-pitched that you have to cover your ears.

And while you stare, the thing begins to swell. It grows and grows until it's as big as a basketball . . . as big as a beachball . . . bigger . . . until it spreads back to the mirror it stepped from, until it swells toward the one you first looked at.

And as it does so, you feel yourself pushed back and back, back and back. You bump into the first mirror but the thing doesn't stop swelling. Within seconds, it's as tall as the hallway, as wide as the distance between the two mirrors.

You feel yourself being mashed, but the thing does not stop. You try to worm your way to the left—but you cannot. You try to move to the right—but you cannot. And slowly you feel yourself being pushed *into* the mirror. But for some strange reason it does not break . . .

Turn to page 109.

98

You try to scream but Golvan is squeezing your head so hard you can make only bubbly, groaning noises. You try to kick him in the stomach, but your toe strikes hard metal plates. You try to slap his arms away, but it's like hitting steel armor.

Still carrying you by the head, he pushes through a partially curtained opening into a terrifying workroom. You see huge blocks of wax, great squares of it! Beyond them, lined against the wall, are small waxed figures. Three of them seem to be moving slightly.

You have a horrifying thought. Inside heavy coatings of wax are other young people, captives of this crazy giant. Those three will soon stop moving!

"No, no, no, no, no . . ." you scream. But it does no good. Golvan walks to a work bench, opens a human-shaped metal box, slams you into it, and bangs the top down. You *know what will happen next!*

You try to scream, but the sound is muffled. You hear something being attached to the box, and you have a good idea what it is. Probably a heavy pipe that will soon be squirting hot liquid wax into this coffinlike thing you're trapped in.

You try to move your arms. You try to move your legs. It's useless. You're trapped. You hear the gurgle of liquid wax. You yell when it splashes on your head and slowly begins to coat you all over . . . and your last thought . . . is that you . . . don't think you'll make . . . a very good . . . wax . . . figure . . .

THE END

You spin around, starting down the tunnel. Little yellow lights illuminate the passageway, but you think you see something ahead and begin walking toward it.

You come to a bend in the tunnel, and there before you is a wide, brightly lighted cave. And you realize why the Tunnel of Love is closed for repairs; a side section has fallen, letting Gulf water flow in. You see no workmen . . .

But you see something else! Half a dozen small Tunnel of Love boats are floating around. In them are mean-looking trolls like the one you saw on the park's midway. They are rowing in zigzag patterns, as if trying to ram and sink one another.

You're so surprised you let out a little cry. Instantly, they all stop rowing, turn, and fix their stares on you. Slowly all raise their oars. One screams, "The enemy! Stop the enemy!"

At once they start rowing toward you! When you try to turn and dash away, you stumble. Before you can regain your footing, they surround you.

"Enemy!" one of them screams. "Intruder!" another shouts. "Spy!" a third one shrieks.

"No!" you yell. "No, I'm not an enemy or spy or—"

But you never finish the sentence. With jabbering cries, they begin beating you over the head with their paddles. And as you slowly sink into the water . . . you wish . . . you'd never come . . . to the Riptide . . . Wonders . . . Park . . .

THE END

100

You do not want to ride the Gravity Whip!

But this witch doesn't care what you want. It plops you into one of the chairs, then it leaps up and lands in your lap!

And at that moment the machine begins to move. At first, you swing side to side, back and forth. But as the huge overhead controlling dish revolves faster and faster, the chairs swing out farther and farther.

The gravity force pins you to the seat. It also makes this witch seem heavier and heavier!

Too heavy!

You hear the calliope, and though you don't recognize the tune, the beat of the music seems to get faster and faster, as if in time to the whirling Gravity Whip.

You're flying straight out. The chains are parallel to the ground. It's then that you hear it, the click and strain of chain links spreading apart—breaking!

Oh, no!

The witch laughs its cackling laugh. The calliope music gets louder and louder.

And you scream!

If you think the chain will break, turn to page 91.
Or does something else happen? Turn to page 95.

"I . . . I'd appreciate your help," you say, keeping your voice low and timid-sounding. "I think I'm a little scared."

101

You hope that by talking softly, you can make the creature think you're really frightened and it'll be gentle with you. After all, you're still pretty sure this is just part of the amusement park's way of making people enjoy its many rides.

But your softer voice does not have the effect you hoped it would. Instead, it seems to make the troll very angry. It suddenly rises, stands in the seat, swings it short arms back and forth, and screams at the top of its shrill voice: *"Nobody makes fun of Toola!"*

Toola, Toola—you didn't mean to make fun of anybody.

But the creature doesn't care what you meant. It begins to jump up and down, making the seat swing violently back and forth. And as it swings, you hear a new and terrifying noise, like all the bolts and hinges creaking and cracking. Before you can do anything to save yourself, the seat you're on suddenly comes apart. The back falls away, the end pieces separate and seem to dangle at the ends of their controlling chains. The rail that's supposed to hold you safely on—it shatters!

And all at once you fall . . .

Turn to page 114.

102

And what you see terrifies you!

You don't know what kind of creature it is. Maybe it's an albatross, maybe it's one of those strange frigate birds, but whatever it is, it's gliding straight at you, its huge wings whirring as it moves. And it makes a horrid hissing noise!

You don't like it—you don't like it all all!

But you can't do anything about it!

The gigantic bird swoops closer, its huge beak wide open. And even as you try to spin yourself away, that terrifying beak closes—around your neck!

And you cease to fall.

You're being carried off . . .

Toward a distant island?

Toward this creature's nest?

You don't know . . . but you are sure of one thing: the farther it take you out over the Gulf of Mexico, the less are your chances of ever—ever—getting back—to that motel . . .

THE END

103

The moment the chair splashes down, you grab the safety bar and cling to it with all your might. You know it will sink for a moment, but you also know it's made of wood and will rise to the surface.

If the searchlight beam has followed you, you're sure it will show just where you are. And if you can float safely for only a few minutes, somebody in a rescue boat will come racing for you.

Within seconds, just as you'd thought, the chair rises to the surface and begins rocking back and forth, up and down, as the waves roll toward the shore.

The searchlight shines on you, its powerful beam cutting a path over the water.

One thing you're certain of: once you're rescued, once you're back on shore, you do not intend to go into another of those crazy houses or climb aboard another ride. You'll go straight to the park's entrance, cross the road, and wait for the bus that will take you back—

Suddenly, your thoughts are interrupted by something that breaks above the waves. At first it makes you think of a wide plank of wood, but when it moves into the searchlight's brilliant beam, you know it is not a length of wood . . .

And your heart almost stops beating when you realize what this thing is!

Turn to page 116.

104

You stand still, holding your breath and listening. But when the noise stops, you decide you're just hearing things and proceed slowly down the hall. You see displays of shells different from any you've ever seen before. Some remind you of sand dollars except they're much larger; some are like long, hollow tubes, twisted in corkscrew shapes; three are as large as frying pans, with small, bottle-shaped ends where, you suppose, sea creatures once lived; several have rainbow colors with what you think are small pearls fixed in the small folds; and one looks like . . .

A skull?

You gasp. *What* is a skull doing here with these shells? Whoever set up this part of the display wasn't thinking, or didn't know shells from bones.

You're about to turn left when you hear the scratching noise once more. Startled because it's louder this time, you look ahead, and spot a narrow doorway that's curtained off by a stained sheet of canvas. Probably, you decide, the entrance to the exhibit workroom, where people get the shells ready for showing.

Again, you hear scratching. It's even louder now, and you decide you don't want to look at these things any longer. You'd rather go try one of the rides.

You're not sure how to go back through the House of Mirrors, though, so you decide to walk through the curtained-off passage. Workmen probably have another way of going in and out.

Turn to page 35.

105

You've heard of sea monsters. You've read about some kind of creature that's supposed to live somewhere in England or Scotland—what's it called?—the Loch Ness monster? Well, whatever, nobody's *really* seen it. And you've watched TV cartoons with sea creatures and huge dragons.

But none of them, not one, looked like this thing moving through the Tunnel of Love.

As it approaches, you understand why the Tunnel of Love is closed. This—this creature has invaded it. It's huge and round and long, reminding you of a snake that's bigger in width than your whole body. Its head is shaped like that of a turtle, but it has bulging, glowing purple eyes, a gaping mouth, and round little ears that lie flat against the sides of its head. And each time it grunts, a long greenish tongue comes slashing out of its mouth.

You press yourself against the tunnel wall, hoping the creature won't see you. But your foot slips on a rock, you twist right, and fall splashing into the shallow water.

The horrid creature stops, its head weaves back and forth, it lets out a terrifying grunt—and that long, slashing tongue swishes from the gaping mouth.

Before you can twist away, the tongue wraps itself around you—and you are jerked toward those gaping jaws.

Your last thought . . . your very last . . . is that you wish you'd gone with Mrs. Howe . . . to see . . . those boats . . .

THE END

106

As it works its way out of the shell, the nautilus swells and shrinks. The more of it that becomes visible, the more terrifying it appears.

Now you understand why this place isn't open to visitors. This thing is alive! The owners of the amusement park probably didn't know that when they put the shell here. And not only is it alive: it's dangerous!

You also know you *do not* want to stay and watch it, or be touched by those slimy feelers.

Very carefully, you take a step backward. The instant you do, those feelers begin swishing up and down, back and forth, humming like giant whips. You swallow hard and take another backward step—and trip over a crack in the floor.

Surprised and shocked, you cry out . . .

The sound puts the giant nautilus in a frenzy. Its body swells and shrinks more violently. The feelers swish back and forth so rapidly they become nothing but a blur. Then suddenly, before you can move, something like a whip lashes you across the shoulder. Another strikes your side.

You scream! *All* at once those feelers whip out like writhing snakes. They wrap themselves about you, squeezing like tightening springs. You again hear that horrid scratching noise as those feelers drag you toward that ugly cone-shaped head, as those glowing eyes seem to burn right through you, and as you're dragged *inside the world's largest shell* . . .

THE END

108

It means that all the power is off, that there are no brakes, and that you'll keep riding and riding until . . .

Until something dreadful happens!

Faster and faster you ride—roaring up hills, down hills, around wicked curves and then back up again. You thunder past the control area, but instead of doing anything to slow you down or stop the car, everybody is looking—just looking, with their hands over their mouths. They cannot believe it—nor can you!

You think about jumping off. But how? And where? If you jump when the car is at the top of one of those loops, it'll come crashing down on you. And if you try to jump while it's going down a hill, you know you cannot move fast enough!

You cry out! Terrified, you wave your arms! But it's all useless—you're stuck in this runaway roller coaster car—and you'll just have to keep riding, riding, riding . . . until something breaks . . . or wears out . . . or the car . . . falls off the track and crashes to earth . . . with you in it . . .

THE END

You feel your breath being squeezed out of your lungs as the thing keeps growing. You wonder how long it can keep swelling that way.

You wonder, too, how long you can live without breathing.

But just when you *know* you're going to be squeezed to death between the thing and the mirror, you realize the mirror surface is also stretching.

It's not glass—it's some kind of plastic. And the more the thing swells, the more the mirror stretches. It pushes you out and out and out, until you feel like you're on the surface of a terribly huge bag of air.

You don't like it. You don't like it at all!

If you can just do something to stop it! Frantically, you twist about and try the only thing you can think of—you jab at the thing with your fingernail.

You hear a quick hiss of air, and all of a sudden the plastic mirror surface splits—and the swelling thing explodes!

You are instantly blasted through the air—over all the rides, over all the concession stands, over the midway and past the kiddie rides. And you scream, knowing that when you finally hit the ground you'll be dashed to death.

Turn to page 45.

110

It smiles a horrid smile. "Flee, child, flee!" it screams. "Or I'll eat . . . you . . . too!"

You need no further urging. Before the swing fully stops, you slide off, drop to the ground, and scurry as fast as you can toward the amusement park entrance. But just as you reach it, you pause long enough to look back.

And what you see terrifies you, sending cold shivers up and down your back. The witch creature is standing up, spreading its cloak like a billowing black sheet. It is grinning an evil grin.

You glance down at its feet—and you want to cry out.

For what moments before had been a man lying on the ground is now nothing more than a bare skeleton!

You know you'll have nightmares the rest of the night . . . the rest of your life—*if* you can get out of the amusement park . . .

THE END

The sound scares you, but you're curious. Cautiously, you proceed to the bend in the hallway and turn left. At once you're in a room with brilliant orange and green flashing lights. Sitting in the center of the room on a low stand is THE SHELL. That sign wasn't kidding; the shell is so huge that the top of it almost touches the ceiling. It is brilliant pearly pink and gray, with little crusty folds along its opening edges shaded blue and green.

You hesitate a moment, then you approach it slowly. When you're within a foot of it, you bend over and put a finger on one of the folds.

Instantly, you hear that horrid scratching sound once more. The whole shell vibrates. Before you have time to step back, a gigantic cone-shaped head oozes its way out of the shell's largest opening. It's black with bulbous orange-glowing eyes. Around what must be its mouth are long feelers.

You've read something about a chambered nautilus and this shell looks like the picture you recall. You knew some kind of animal lived in the shell. But this *big!*

The scratching noise gets louder as those long feelers flick against the shell's crusty folds. You tremble all over as that horrible-looking head keeps moving about, and as those glowing eyes fix their stare on you!

Turn to page 106.

112

Your scream has an instantaneous, terrifying effect. For no sooner does the sound escape your lips than all the creatures, the one alone and the six others at the other side, swell up like rapidly blown balloons. They stretch and grow until they blend into one massive air bag . . .

And explode!

The force of the explosion blows the roof off the House of Mirrors, sends fragments of broken glass showering out on all the people in the amusement park, and blasts you up and out of there.

You yell but nobody seems to care! You cry out that you need help, but nobody listens!

You fly in an arc over most of the rides, and when you start down, you know you'll crash headlong onto the kiddies' merry-go-round.

But even as you think it, something suddenly snags you, and you're caught in mid-air—caught and dangling. The suddenness of your capture startles you and you try to turn about. You cannot move easily, but when you are able to see, you realize that you've landed on that thing called the Sky Chase, some kind of cable car ride.

You don't want another ride; all you want is to get down!

Turn to page 63.

You also hear heavy footsteps. And a deep, low laugh. It's that giant creature—he's coming for you.

You glance upward, toward the box's lid. But all of it does not open. Instead, a small door is swung back, and in the dim light that filters through, you see the outline, not of the giant, but of some little four-legged creatures with huge jaws and long, swishing tails . . .

"Mealtime, my pretties," you hear the giant say, laughing softly all the while.

And those four-legged creatures with their long, swishing tails and wide, wide jaws drop into the box, one by one.

You know what they are. You've seen them in the Everglade zoos and in documentary films about south Florida: they're young—and very hungry—alligators!

You scream. You holler for the giant to let you out!

He only laughs again, drops in the last of the dozen young 'gators and closes the trap door.

You know if it's mealtime for them, you're the meal . . .

THE END

114

. . . But just when you're certain you'll drop into the machinery that operates this Triple Spin ferris wheel, those long, dreadful claws of the troll hook themselves into the back of your shirt . . .

And they stretch!

Like powerful rubber bands, they stretch and stretch and stretch—all the way down to the ground. And you land gently in soft sand, very safe and well away from the ferris wheel motor.

At once, the claws release you and spring back up all the way to the troll's hand.

Crazy, crazy, crazy—but you don't care. You're safe, you're on the ground, and nobody's holding you. With only a very brief glance back, you whirl around and dash toward the entrance of Riptide Wonders. You made a mistake, you should have gone with Mrs. Howe and the others to see boats. Maybe you don't care about them at all but you're sure they'd be a lot safer than *this* crazy place.

Right now all you want to do is catch the bus back to the motel . . . where you'll be safe . . . and you won't have to worry about things like ferris wheels and crazy mirror houses . . . and trolls . . .

THE END

And he carries you through a curtain at the re.. the room. In pain and agony, you look about. T... you see the other creatures—the troll-like midget, ... witch, and the clown. The midget begins jumping up and down, the clown laughs, and the witch cackles. *"Now!"* it screeches. *"Now* we can have our pet!"

"Our pet!" You don't understand. But whatever they have in mind, you know you won't like it. The three of them begin to move toward a huge table in the center of this strange work place. And on the table is the skin of a young alligator—tail, huge jaws, wicked teeth and all. You can see that its body is about your size——

Your size?

The witch and the clown turn the skin, belly-side up, while the troll leaps onto the table. He grabs a huge needle threaded with black string. And you *know* what they intend doing with you.

You scream and struggle, but it's useless. Handling you as if you're nothing more than a rag doll, Golvan turns you about and slams you down onto the table.

You kick and swing your arms. "I don't like it!" you scream. But the clown laughs, the witch cackles, and the troll jumps up and down. And the three of them help Golvan *stuff you into the 'gator's skin.* And he holds you there while the troll sews you inside it!

And you know . . . as he makes the final stitch . . . that you won't get back . . . to the motel . . . because you'll be . . . the pet of these . . . evil four . . .

THE END

116

A sawfish!

You've seen creatures like it on television. Its snout is very long, like a woodman's crosscut saw. You've seen sea beasts like it ram that snout through the bottom of lifeboats, cutting the thing in half and sawing into passengers.

You know the sawfish is big; you'd read that they can sometimes grow to be twenty feet long.

And this one is coming straight at you and the Gravity Whip chair!

You yell, you scream, you kick your feet, trying to turn or row the seat. But you cannot overcome the force of the waves.

The sawfish swims closer, its long, sharp-toothed snout rising out of the water like a powerful blade.

You hear the low roar of a rescue boat's motor as someone rushes to your aid. But the boat is at least fifty yards away, and the sawfish is less than ten feet . . . no, less than eight feet . . . no, less than five feet . . . no, less than three feet.

You raise both feet, getting them out of the water. You kick at the snout. Wildly you swing both arms about, hoping to knock it off its path.

But it moves straight at the seat . . . it bumps the wood . . . its saw teeth slice through the wood as if it were nothing more than a jellyfish . . . and you feel those teeth . . . slicing . . . into . . . you . . . and you scream . . . one last time . . .

THE END

For a split second all motion seems to stop. The tower becomes very still and you hope you're wrong about it breaking from the base.

But before you can feel anything like relief, it slowly begins to fall—away from the Gulf.

At first, you think it will go slowly down, kept from a fast fall by those huge steel cables that should keep it steady. But you hear one cable snap, then another, then a third and fourth. And with each cracking snap you seem to be falling faster. You hear people on the ground screaming. You glance down and see everybody scurrying out of the way. Nobody can stop the tower.

But you're not ready to be crushed by this monstrous thing. You look wildly about, then you make up your mind. You set yourself, release your grip on the safety rail, and spring out as hard as you can. If you've got to crash, you don't want that thing on top of you.

You tumble over and over, and when you look where you're going, you realize you're headed for one of the food concessions. You close your eyes . . .

And when you hit, everything goes splat!

But when you stop moving, you realize you weren't crushed to death. You freeze for a moment, then take a deep breath. You smell something very sweet, and you know where you've fallen. You're mired almost at the very bottom—of the world's largest container of cotton candy . . .

THE END

118

But it's sweet, so very sweet. You think breathing the perfume is as good as eating candy. And the farther you walk, the more of it you smell. You cannot help yourself, you want to smell more and more . . .

Suddenly you stop walking because you don't believe what you see. Large plants along the walkway seem to be moving, as if stirred by a soft breeze. But there's no breeze. Yet they move. And not only do they move, they grow. Right there before your eyes, they grow!

The perfumed air is now so thick it's stinging your eyes. You blink, and when you stare ahead again, those plants with their gigantic leaves and long, ropelike stems keep growing and growing. And the nearer you get to them, the more rapidly they spread.

You're fascinated. You've never seen living plants actually grow. You squint your eyes, you sniff. And without thinking about it, you stretch out a hand, just to touch one of those stems.

You shouldn't have!

For the moment your finger comes in contact with it, the stem, like a wild and crazy spring, suddenly coils itself about your arm. It grows ever more rapidly. The plant next to it also seems to grow. Their stems combine, and they wrap themselves slowly about the arm, then about your waist, then about your shoulders, and finally around your neck.

You've read about plants like these—but you didn't believe it. Now, though . . . as they choke you . . . you know that there really are . . . man-eating . . . plants . . .

THE END